PURPOSEFUL ACTION

7 Steps to Fulfillment

Towanna B. Freeman, CEC, DD
Barbara H. Pellegrino, CEC

iUniverse, Inc.
New York Bloomington

The information, ideas, and suggestions in this book are not intended as a substitute for professional advice. Before following any suggestions contained in this book, you should consult your personal physician or mental health professional. Neither the author nor the publisher shall be liable or responsible for any loss or damage allegedly arising as a consequence of your use or application of any information or suggestions in this book.

iUniverse books may be ordered through booksellers or by contacting:

iUniverse
1663 Liberty Drive
Bloomington, IN 47403
www.iuniverse.com
1-800-Authors (1-800-288-4677)

Because of the dynamic nature of the Internet, any Web addresses or links contained in this book may have changed since publication and may no longer be valid. The views expressed in this work are solely those of the author and do not necessarily refl ect the views of the publisher, and the publisher hereby disclaims any responsibility for them.

ISBN: 978-1-4401-6387-6 (sc)
ISBN: 978-1-4401-6388-3 (ebook)
ISBN: 978-1-4401-6389-0 (hc)

Printed in the United States of America

Cover design by EJDesign Firm, LLC.

iUniverse rev. date: 10/05/2009

Table of Contents

Acknowledgments

To my parents, Clarence and Melissa Burrous, for preparing me.

To my grandmother, Mrs. Estelle Burrous, and my departed grandfather, Mr. Thomas Burrous, thank you for teaching me to be strong in the face of adversity.

To my beautiful daughter, Jenny Harper, who keeps me laughing and loves me unconditionally.

To my mentor and friend, Norman Bailey, who saw something in me I hadn't seen myself, and who has traveled with me on my path to discovering my full potential.

To Dr. Bruce D. Schneider, founder of the world-renowned iPEC Coach Training School and the iPEC family of coaches.

Most of all, to my husband, Byron Freeman, for your love, constant encouragement, and support that helped make my vision for this book a reality.

Love, Towanna

Acknowledgments

To my mother, June Tenenbaum, a living miracle, who has always been the driving force behind everything I have done.

To my husband, Dr. Rand Pellegrino. When I met him I thought all my dreams had come true. Little did I know that he would introduce me to much bigger and better dreams many times over.

To Dr. Towanna Freeman, who is living proof that synchronicity is reality.

To my loyal and loving family and friends, who have believed in me since day one.

To all my students who continue to use the Vision Board and Mind Skills program to achieve their dreams and goals. You continually show me that this system works for anyone who applies the practices.

To all of you, thank you. To your continued success.

Love, Barbara

Introduction

We are so delighted and excited that you have decided to take the necessary first steps to make some wonderful changes in your life. No matter what stage of life you are in, Purposeful Action is designed to help you recognize and reprioritize your life goals and work on what is really important to you - your heart's desire, your passion. You may want to change careers, to be closer to your family, to become a millionaire, to lose weight, or to feel better about yourself. Whatever the reason you have decided to take this journey, if you want to make your vision a reality, and use a proven method that has worked for so many others, we ask that you focus your attention on what you really desire deep inside your heart.

How Towanna and Barbara Met

Being in the right place at the right time can help fulfill your destiny. That is what happened the day I met Barbara Pellegrino. Who would think that Barbara Pellegrino, a Caucasian woman from Australia, and Towanna Freeman, an African American woman from Washington, DC, would meet and team up? But we did. In September 2008, we both lived in Hawaii and were focused on our coaching practices. The initial curiosity and draw for each other was compelling, and we just had to get to know each other. In just three months, our friendship deepened to a level that only best friends with years of history attain.

We shared our life experiences, business acumen, and specialized skills.

While exploring Barbara's mind power life skills from Hawaii and the Land Down Under, and my life-planning skills and stately East Coast work ethic, we discovered our purpose for connecting. Like magic, we became a dream team. We conversed, laughed, and cried over tea, coffee, lunch, and snacks. New ideas and inspiration flowed easily, and projects were joyfully created and masterfully crafted.

Barbara's Story

In 1977, I was awarded a diploma in fashion design and production, and I began my career in the Australian clothing industry. I quickly moved up the corporate ladder from designer into the buying and importing side of the profession, and I was (at that time) the youngest clothing buyer in Australia to travel overseas. I thoroughly enjoyed the rag trade - the work, the glamour, and the travel - but after eight years, I was wondering what else life had to offer.

In 1985, I discovered the personal development world and began to take even greater control of my life and destiny by learning about the mind and the law of attraction. I became certified as a neuro-linguistic programming (NLP) facilitator and trainer, and I utilized all these skills to achieve greater goals and a more balanced life.

In 1994, I experienced the greatest result of my personal development work. I met and married my husband, Rand, moved to Hawaii, and began to live a life bigger and better than what I had envisioned.

One morning in 2005, I woke up wondering how it happened that I was consistently living a life beyond my greatest of dreams. As I backtracked through my experiences, I considered that I had efficiently utilized the personal development skills that I had studied and taught while living in Australia.

Being with Rand in Hawaii had deepened the spiritual aspects within me. I was truly living and walking the talk. I knew that I had a winning formula; it was not luck. I had a formula for success, and I decided to share it so that other people could follow this proven process to achieve their dreams and desires. The formula can be summarized as "Vision Boards," and the results are profound. In 2006, I created and began teaching workshops on Vision Boards: "Treasure Mapping Your Way to Success."

Meeting Towanna in 2008 began another new, creative, and exciting adventure, and it has proven to be a wonderful friendship. We hope that many, many people will benefit from the fruits of our friendship, living the lives of their greatest dreams through practical, purposeful, and inspired action.

Towanna's Story

I lived in corporate America for over a decade, specializing in project management. I developed proven leadership and management skills by developing and implementing successful leadership, diversity inclusion, team building, and strategic change initiatives. I built a strong corporate identity of which I was extremely proud.

In 1999, I founded the Young Women's Empowerment Network (YWEN), a nonprofit organization dedicated to helping future leaders of America. My small workshops grew into a six-city tour, where thousands of young women across the United States have participated in leadership training workshops and conferences. YWEN was a huge success, and I was proud of the work we were accomplishing. However, volunteering and running the nonprofit was strictly a part-time passion because I was afraid to let go of my corporate identity. By most standards, I was extremely successful. I was making top dollar, had a beautiful home, and vacationed in exotic places. Corporate America was my security blanket.

I married my husband and became an army wife in 2007, and one year later, the army moved my family to Hawaii. Since I had lived in the Washington, DC area all my life, I was up for a change - as long as I could bring my corporate identity with me. The perfect plan was in motion: I would move to Hawaii, and because of advances in Internet technology, nothing had to change. At least, that is what I believed.

I had no idea that the move to Hawaii would be the most significant turning point in my professional, spiritual, and personal life.

Although unexpected, the economic downturn of 2008 was what inspired me to act on my choice to leave corporate America, and it was an amicable separation. It was during my quiet times at the beach that I realized that my most gratifying accomplishments were rooted in my nonprofit work.

My passion was to inspire the next generation of leaders. At this point, I recognized a strong commitment to help women who were searching for more fulfillment, as I was.

My decision to separate from corporate America was a significant one. However, I was willing to take the risk. I desired more than a corporate identity; I desired fulfillment. No, it was not easy, but I turned my feelings of loss and sadness into excitement and curiosity for a new opportunity. With my purpose in mind, I prayed daily for my success, I planned my activities each week, and I pursued the vision I had for my life. I have used this routine all my life, and it works.

Coming Together

Everything has a purpose, and purposeful action is the ability to visualize and realize what you want, when you want it, and how you want it. So Barbara and I decided to combine our strengths, talents, and best practices in order to share our success formulas with you.

This book is designed to carefully and efficiently guide you through the process of creating a purposeful plan of action for your life. As professional life and success coaches, we will guide you through a process of self-discovery that we have learned, experienced, and successfully taught to others.

To get the most out of this process, we have included checklists, exercises, and most importantly, the six key questions that have helped our clients live more fulfilled lives:

1. What will make you happy?

2. What event brought you to this decision?

3. What are your strengths and opportunities?

4. What can prevent you from achieving your goal?

5. What are your personal investments?

6. When do you want to accomplish this goal?

While creating your plan, you will focus your conscious mind, change limiting beliefs, and help reprogram your subconscious mind with empowering thoughts to move you forward and achieve your goals in the shortest time and most efficient manner.

What Will Make You Happy?

Women are excelling in every career imaginable. They are strong, independent, and sexually liberated. However, with all our successes, there has been a great sacrifice. Over the last three decades, women have been working longer hours, raising children as a single parent, juggling the needs of the household and the demands of a career, having longer commutes to the office and less time for friends and family. And still women desire to have more, do more, and be more in their lifetimes.

There is nothing unusual or unhealthy about the desire to have more success. So what is success? In simple terms, success is successfully completing what you plan to do. It could mean purchasing a new car, getting a new job, finishing graduate school, getting married, living healthier, getting a makeover, or making more money. There is nothing complicated or confusing about it. When you make a plan and follow the plan, you will achieve success in whatever you plan to do.

However, when most people seek success, what they are really seeking is fulfillment. What is fulfillment? Fulfillment is to do, be, and have what you want, on your terms, according to what is in your heart. It is being satisfied with what you have because it is what you chose, not what someone else chose for you. You see, if you are not happy, content, or pleased with what you have,you are not living the vision you have for your life.

It does not matter if you are independently wealthy or living from paycheck to paycheck. If you are not fulfilled, you are not living the vision you have for your life, and you are probably ignoring what you feel in your heart. Your vision for your life is a mental image of something that is not apparent in your reality. Your vision for your life is what will cause you to jump out of bed in the morning instead of waking up with anxiety.

People who are not living the vision for their lives will get out of bed tomorrow and do the same thing they did today: do the same work, see the same people, and complain about the same things. They work to make money, to spend money, just to be forced to make money again. And then the next day, the cycle repeats itself. Day after day, week after week, year after year, and all of a sudden, life will be over. Without vision or knowing how to attain your vision, you are simply living, working, and existing beneath your true potential.

You were born with an innate vision. Your vision for your life helps you understand why you exist ... and what you were put on earth to accomplish. With the knowledge of why you exist, you can determine what you want and develop a plan of action to succeed.

To help you walk you through this first step of self-discovery, allow us to introduce you to Nicole and Carol. They are two coaching clients who decided it was time to live the life they'd always envisioned for themselves. We will reference them throughout the book to show you how they applied the process to their lives.

Case Study: Nicole

Nicole is a successful executive, mother, and divorcée. She has spent fifteen years establishing her career and nurturing her small family as a single parent.

She works a forty-hour week, and her children have a busy sports and recreation routine on the weekends. Nicole volunteers her time in her community and goes to church on Sundays. She has single-handedly secured a comfortable lifestyle for herself and her children.

Nichole achieved great success by acquiring what she wanted. In fact, there were days when her acquisitions appeared without any effort on her part. However, Nicole's journey to success was not an easy one. She divorced her husband when her children were ages two and four. As a newly single parent with two children, Nicole lived just above poverty. There were months when she had to decide whether to pay bills or buy groceries to feed her family.

One year after her divorce, it became apparent to Nicole that if she wanted to achieve more in life, she needed to change careers to increase her household income.

She was college educated, but she needed additional skills for the career change. With a plan in mind and determination in her heart, Nicole accomplished her goal. Within five years of her divorce, Nicole had changed careers, doubled her income, and purchased a home and a new car.

Nicole is very proud of her personal success. She loves providing for her family and loves spending time with them. However, for many years, Nicole has lived a predictable life. Nicole is overcommitted and stressed with the activities for her job, her children, and her community.

Whenever Nicole talks to her fun-loving friends, she feels envious of their lifestyles. If her friends are on a romantic vacation getaway, she wishes to be there. If they are out dancing, she wishes to be there. If they are at a day spa, she wishes to be there. Nicole wants more fun, excitement, and romance in her life. She wants to tell adventurous stories to her friends versus living vicariously through them.

Although she wants all these things, Nicole feels she can never change her life routine because her children would feel neglected. She believes she needs to focus solely on the happiness of her children. Their happiness and security has been her primary focus.

Case Study: Carol

Carol is twenty-eight years old and has worked in a prestigious law firm as an executive assistant for five years.

She has a loving boyfriend and a supportive family who continue to encourage her to follow her dreams.

As a college student, Carol dreamed of owning her own day spa, and she has the education and entrepreneurial mindset to do so. However, she lacks the time and energy to develop her business plan fully. The demand of the law firm keeps Carol in the office for ten to twelve hours each day. When Carol comes home from work, she is too tired to think about her dream career.

In fact, she has put away her journals that outline her business plan. Monday through Friday, Carol starts her day at five o'clock in the morning, with a one-hour commute. On her way home from work, Carol grabs fast food for dinner and arrives home between seven and nine o'clock.

To make matters worse, Carol has progressively gained twenty pounds from this hectic work schedule and poor eating habits. When life was considered normal for Carol, she would come home from work around five o'clock, go to the gym, and make a healthy dinner for herself.

The only free time Carol has is on the weekends or holidays when the office is closed. She dedicates this time to her boyfriend, whom she has been dating for four years.

Carol says they plan to marry one day, but not until her life gets back on track.

To stay connected to her dream of owning a day spa, Carol and her boyfriend plan vacations to popular cities in North America and Canada. While on vacation, Carol visits the best day spas the city has to offer.

Each vacation renews her entrepreneurial passion, making it easy for Carol to recall her mission statement: To help clients refresh, recharge, and nurture the mind, body, and spirit.

Unfortunately, the fun from the vacation wears off when Carol returns to work. Within a week, Carol is depressed and feels like a failure because she realizes she is not living the vision for her life. Carol desires a change in her life.

Now it is your turn to introduce yourself by completing the chapter exercises. When you connect with your innate vision, you will unlock your full potential in every area of your life. Remember, your vision is what motivates you. Only when you decide to take action to bring your vision into your reality will you develop a clear and concise plan.

Step 1.1: What do you dream of having or accomplishing?

Step 1.2: What would make you happy?

Reflection

Your action plan is your pathway to purpose, leading you to your life of happiness, contentment, and fulfillment.

What Event Brought You to This Decision?

To live the vision for your life, you must know yourself - who you are on the inside. You know, the person you are when no one is looking at you; your private thoughts about yourself; your thoughts that would shock a crowd if heard out loud. Answers to questions like this: Are you afraid to take risks? Do you hate crowds? Do you like people? Do you prefer to be alone? Do you need to be in control? Do you hate intimacy? Do you want to please people?

This second step in creating a plan of action is to identify your current view of yourself so that you can make any necessary changes. It is important to identify any personal fears, limiting beliefs, or negative behaviors that will prevent you from accomplishing your goals.

Nicole and Carol were asked similar questions in a coaching session, and this is what they said.

Case Study: Nicole

Towanna: *Nicole, what will make you happy?*

Nicole: *Besides seeing my children smile and laugh every day, having more fun and excitement in my personal life would make me happy.*

Towanna: *What events in your life brought you to this decision?*

Nicole: *A few months ago, I attended my high school reunion. Initially, I was not planning to go because I didn't have a date. However, when I found out that one of my friends was going alone, we partnered up and went together. I had such a great time! I felt as if a veil had been lifted off my face, and I was alive and relevant.*

Towanna: *What kind of person do you want to be?*

Nicole: *I want to be a person who not only takes care of her family, but also finds time to relax and enjoy life every day. I need to take time for myself.*

Towanna: *What kind of person does Nicole have to become in order to live the life she envisions?*

Nicole: *I have to be a person who is open to making changes in her life. I have to be a person who spends less time controlling life and more time living it freely.*

Case Study: Carol

Towanna: *What will make Carol happy?*

Carol: *Owning a day spa and losing twenty*

pounds would make me happy.

Towanna: *How much of your life are you willing to change to make this happiness a reality?*

Carol: *It sounds so easy when I say it. However, I want a total life makeover. I want to make changes in my life even though it will be tough.*

Towanna: *What kind of person do you want to be?*

Carol: *I want to be a person who has more control over her life.*

Towanna: *What kind of person does Carol have to become in order to live the life she envisions?*

Carol: *I have to be a person of focus and determination. I have to be a person who is not afraid to make changes in her life.*

It is your turn again to be open and honest about your current view of your life. You may need additional time to gather your thoughts before writing your answers.

Step 2.1: What are your strengths?

____

____

____

____

____

____

Step 2.2: What event in your life brought you to this decision to follow your vision?

Step 2.3: To activate your vision, what strengths would you add to your list?

Life Balance

When your life is overrun with busy activities and is cluttered with one project after another, it is understandable and normal that you feel overwhelmed. You may find yourself not focusing on areas of your life that are important.

There is nothing wrong with having focus and determination to get things done. However, when your projects and activities lead to signs of an unbalanced life with feelings of frustration and chronic stress, it is time to assess your priorities and values in order to put things back into balance. Nicole and Carol are both experiencing signs of an unbalanced life:

❍ Feeling overwhelmed

❍ A change in appetite

❍ Feelings of guilt

❍ Continual sadness

❍ Lack of sleep

Step 2.4: Which of these signs are you experiencing? Go over them again and check ones that apply to you.

It is not easy to notice when your life gets out of balance, as it is usually a gradual progression of one sacrifice after another. You are taking less time for yourself and falling behind in various duties, while trying to do more, usually for others.

However, identifying the signs is the first step to realizing that your life might be more like a rat race - running in a self-defeating, exhausting, and unfulfilling race that is not taking you anywhere near your full potential.

Now that you have examples of how your life gets out of balance, let us look at a few behaviors of an unbalanced life:

❍ You have too many demands in your life - spreading yourself too thin.

❍ Your priorities are not in order.

❍ You do not communicate effectively.

❍ You are not satisfied with the simple things.

❍ You have unrealistic expectations.

❍ You spend more time performing unproductive tasks than productive ones.

Step 2.5: Review again the example behaviors of an unbalanced life. Check ones that apply to you.

Step 2.6: What is preventing you from having more balance in your life?

Step 2.7: Envision a life of balance - where you are less stressed, where you have enough time to get things done, where you are at peace. Write down the things you could accomplish:

It is okay to have mixed emotions about your list. It may feel frustrating to look at, or you may be breathing a sigh of relief because you finally needed to admit that you no longer want to, nor have to, be superwoman every day. And you may find it comforting to discover that you are not alone, and that there is guidance and support to achieve a better future.

Meditation Exercise: take a minute to quiet your mind. Take a deep breath and exhale slowly to the count of four: one ... two ... three ... four ... Repeat two more times. Imagine your body relaxing. Let the tension flow from your body into the floor. Now let positive images come into your awareness - imagines of things that are beautiful and peaceful. Feel the positive energy and see yourself smiling and laughing.

Reflection

Many people spend many years seeking direction for their lives. The turning point comes when you begin to believe that within yourself are the ingredients for accomplishing your goals and seeing your vision become reality.

If you want happiness, contentment, and fullfilment, the only obstacle on your journey is your lack of action. Otherwise, if you believe in your natural abilities, you will be unstoppable.

Life Balance Wheel

What is it?

The Life Balance Wheel is an assessment tool designed to help you discover your overall balance, satisfaction levels, and current perception of your life. Doing this exercise will enable you to make informed and clear decisions about the areas of your life you wish to improve. This is an extremely powerful tool for gaining control and developing your personal power.

Life Balance Wheel

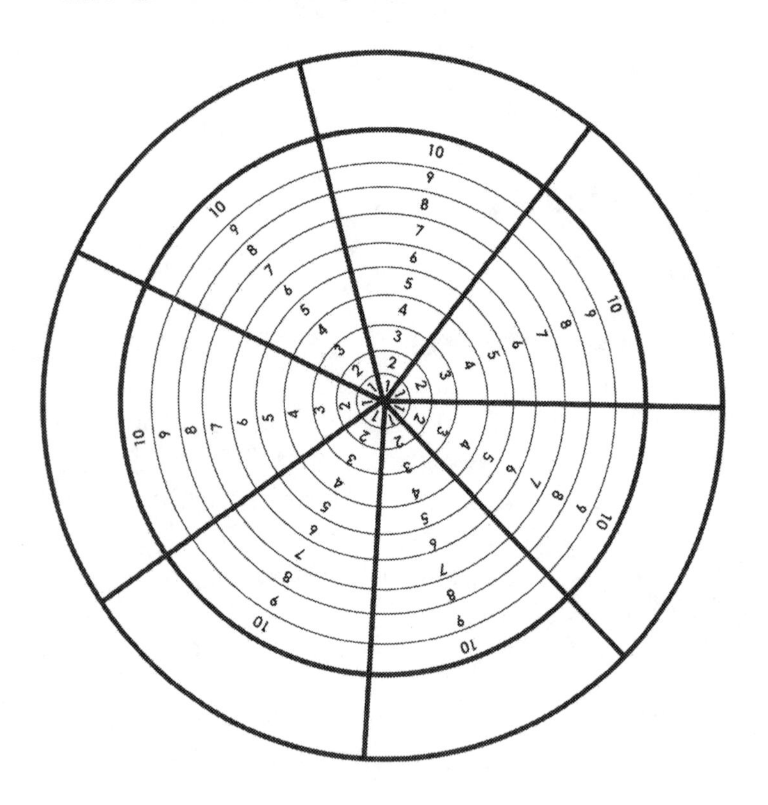

Life Balance Wheel

The Life Balance Wheel can be customized to reflect different areas of your life. For Nicole and Carol, the following areas were added to the wheel:

- Family
- Career and job
- Fun and recreation
- Money
- Health and fitness
- Relationship
- Personal growth and spirituality

Here are other areas used in the Life Balance Wheel:

- Love
- Education
- Environment
- Community involvement
- Values
- Spouse

You can also use the Life Balance Wheel to review your life roles:

- Mother
- Daughter
- Sister
- Neighbor
- Spouse
- Co-worker
- Extended family

Let us return to our case studies. Both Nicole and Carol completed a Life Balance Wheel during their coaching sessions. In the following diagrams, you will notice how each wheel is a reflection of their discussions in chapter 2.

Case Study: Nicole

Nicole's wheel reveals that fun and recreation has the lowest rating and money the highest rating. In Nicole's case, she desires to have more fun and excitement in her life, while balancing work and family.

Life Balance Wheel

Case Study: Nicole

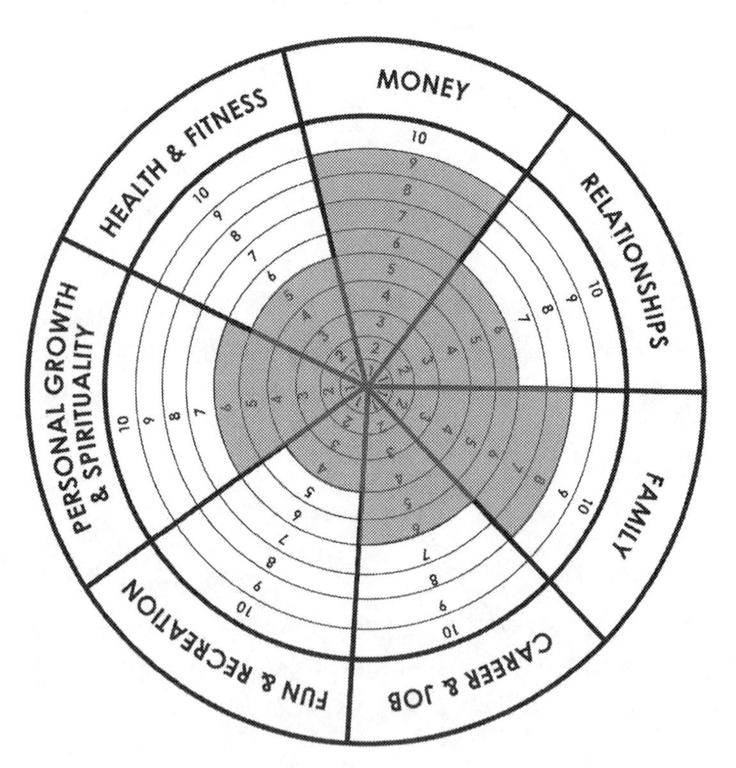

Case Study: Carol

Carol's Life Balance Wheel reveals high ratings in relationships and family. However, career and job has the lowest ratings. In Carol's case, she desires to be in charge of her own time, have a fulfilling career, and feel fit and healthy again.

Life Balance Wheel

Case Study: Carol

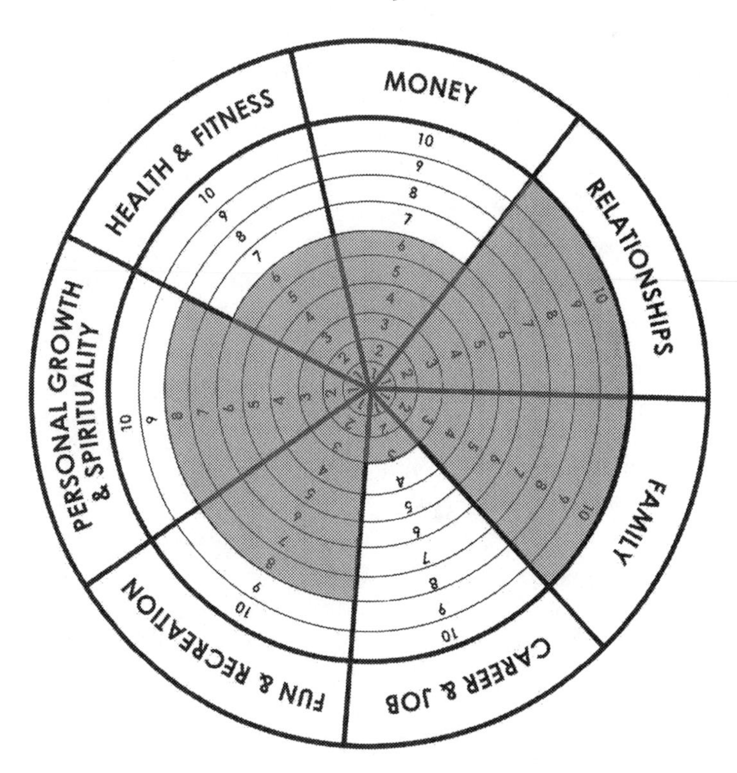

Like Nicole and Carol, consider the same seven areas of life to assess how things are currently in your life. In the following exercise (step 3:1), rate your level of satisfaction for the following areas of your life on a scale of 1 to 10, with 1 being very dissatisfied, and 10 being very satisfied.

For example, if you are completely satisfied with your performance, rate yourself a 10; if you are 50 percent satisfied, rate yourself a 5. This review will allow you to choose the areas you want to work on.

Step 3.1: Rate your level of satisfaction for the following areas of your life on a scale of 1 to 10, with 1 being very dissatisfied, and 10 being very satisfied.

Family
1 2 3 4 5 6 7 8 9 10

Career and Job
1 2 3 4 5 6 7 8 9 10

Fun and Recreation
1 2 3 4 5 6 7 8 9 10

Money
1 2 3 4 5 6 7 8 9 10

Health and Fitness
1 2 3 4 5 6 7 8 9 10

Relationship
1 2 3 4 5 6 7 8 9 10

Personal Growth and Spirituality
1 2 3 4 5 6 7 8 9 10

Transfer Your Scores

1. After you have scored all seven areas, transfer your score to the following Life Balance Wheel.
2. Circle each score and connect the dots on the axis to assess your overall level of satisfaction.
3. When completed, this diagram will give you a good idea of how balanced you feel your life is.

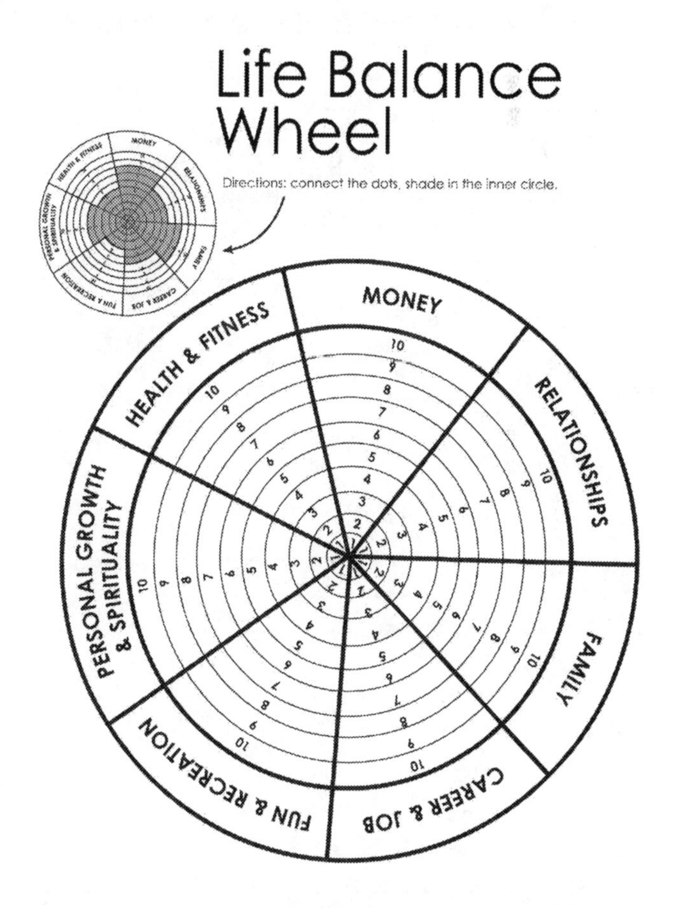

Step 3.2: As you review your results of your Life Balance Wheel, ask yourself the following questions:

How is it riding through life on a wheel that looks like this?

____

____

____

____

Is the ride: smooth, a little rough, or really bumpy?

____

Are some aspects of my life more satisfying and rewarding than others? If so, which aspects?

____

____

____

____

Is there overall balance in my life? Yes or No

What is missing in my life right now?

____

____

____

____

Is something getting *too much* of my attention?

____

____

____

____

Is something getting *too little* of my attention?

____

____

____

____

Step 3.3: Choose which area of your life you will work on first, and then later you will decide which you will work on second, third, and so on.

Area 1: ______________________________________

____

____

____

Area 2: ______________________________________

____

____

____

Area 3: ______________________________________

____

____

____

The information from the Life Balance Wheel will transfer to chapter 8, where you will begin goal setting. Continue to work through each page, giving thought to each of the questions and exercises. The more thought and effort you put into this book, the more you will achieve. This is *Purposeful Action*.

What Are Your Strengths and Opportunities

Many people never fully utilize or recognize their natural strengths and potential because they have not found the proper way to express them in the world. Recognized or not, we all have strengths and potential that make us unique. You were born with purpose, and you have the ability to determine your level of success by making decisions for your life.

The key to your success is controlling negative thoughts, and ultimately your behavior, so that you can take steps toward making your vision a reality. To accomplish this, you should understand the differences between the conscious and subconscious mind.

The Conscious Mind

The conscious mind, or ego, is the part of the mind that is responsible for logic and reasoning, and it is running a constant commentary on your life.

The conscious mind deals with your outside environment by using your five senses as your feed-back. The conscious mind sets goals and judges results. The conscious mind is great at analyzing, organizing, and making decisions, but it is lim-ited in getting results because it involves only 10 percent of the mind's power.

The conscious mind can be compared to a sentinel. The sentinel's purpose is to keep you safe and protected in the reality of what already exists. So, when you think of a new business venture or come up with an idea to improve your life, the sentinel could start to give you all the logical reasons why a new venture would not succeed or why you should not try to improve your life. If it involves risk, the sentinel is there to guard and protect you from an apparently negative outcome.

Your conscious mind is extremely powerful, yet, as you can see, it is not always on your side. It is the voice that is always talking to you, telling you what is good and bad, right and wrong, always judging and commenting on the events of your life. The conscious mind is often referred to as the "chat-terbox," which is essentially a derogatory term.

So that the thoughts are more supportive, we would like to reframe the thoughts - or, in other words, *change* - the way the chatterbox thoughts are presented. As you observe your mind, you will begin to understand that the conscious mind - and the thoughts you are automatically thinking - is not necessarily correct, although it may sound correct.

Most people believe that their thoughts happen automatically, and that they are "just thinking." In reality, you can take absolute control over what you think and, eventually, how you are feeling. You can train your mind to think the thoughts you choose, which will influence your thoughts. It is important that you start to take control and choose your thoughts wisely.

As a man thinks in his heart, so is he (Proverbs 23:7). What a powerful scripture from the Bible! That scripture is a universal principle that many people misinterpret. Most people understand it to mean that as a man thinks, so is he. However, the key words that are missing in that thinking are "in his heart." Your thoughts are connected to your heart. If you believe in your heart that you are not capable of doing what you envision, you will not achieve your goals. If you think you are not ready to live an abundant and purposeful life, you will not do it.

As stated in the last chapter, you were born with a vision for this life. Your vision is what makes you jump out of bed to start your day. So, living your life according to what you see challenges your thoughts and your feelings about yourself in your heart.

Mind Model

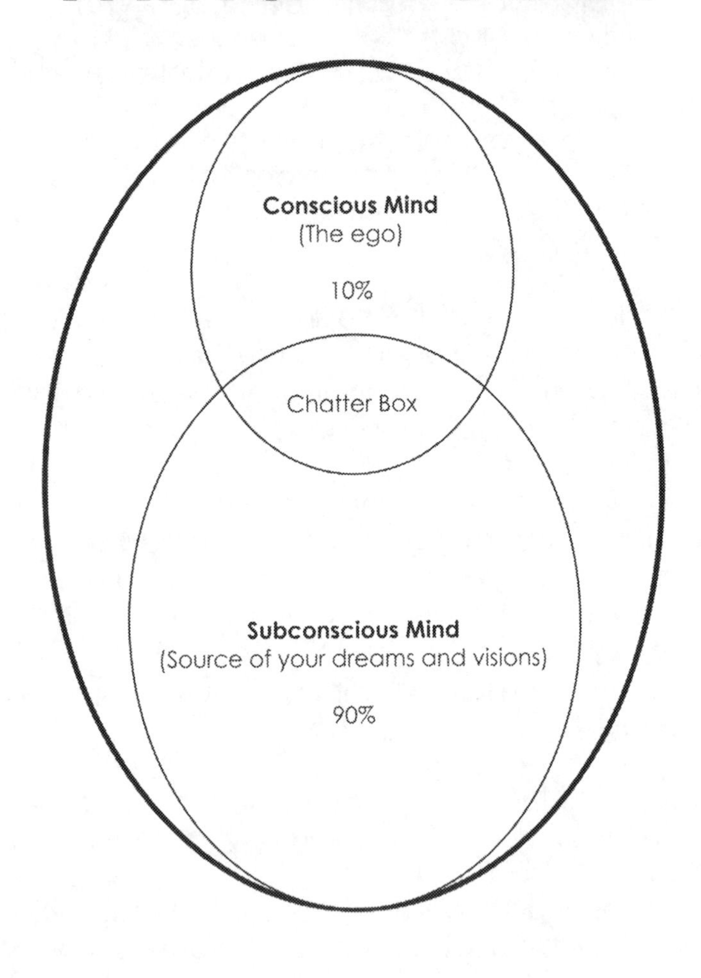
Conscious Mind
(The ego)
10%
Chatter Box
Subconscious Mind
(Source of your dreams and visions)
90%

The Subconscious Mind

The subconscious mind is your "automatic pilot," the part of your mind that is responsible for all your involuntary actions, such as your digestion, your heartbeat, and your breathing rate. Your subconscious mind is also the storage room for all your beliefs and memories. However, the subconscious mind does not know the difference between what is real and what is vividly imagined.

For example, imagine that you are holding a lemon in your hand and then raising your hand in front of your face to see the lemon. Notice the color, texture, and smell. Now, imagine putting the lemon down, cutting the lemon, squeezing the juice, and tasting the sour pulp.

Did you notice something? What inevitably happens is that most people will start to salivate, which is an involuntary action, even though the lemon was not real, only imagined. The subconscious mind that causes the salivation to occur cannot tell the difference between what is real and what is vividly imagined.

As you are doing the exercises in this book, you will use your imagination to imprint new ideas, possibilities, and circumstances into your subconscious mind, which will then compel and propel you toward those events in reality, almost as if you are on autopilot.

Another example is someone learning how to drive. At the beginning of the learning process, the driver cannot hold a conversation with anyone while driving—she can only focusing on newly learned driving skills. However, over time, the driver becomes more experienced, and the driving process becomes automatic. The driver can hold conversations with others in the car and talk on the telephone while driving. The driving skills are transferred to the subconscious mind, and the conscious mind is free to do other things.

In both analogies (tasting the lemon and the new driver), you will notice that the subconscious has no will of its own. It takes instruction from the conscious mind. Despite the fact that the conscious mind is only responsible for 10 percent of the mind's power, it plays the important role of giving commands to the subconscious mind.

Let us now revisit our case studies of Nicole and Carol as they notice their negative thoughts and start to take charge, reprogram, and focus their powerful minds.

Case Study: Nicole

Review: Nicole loves providing for her family and loves spending time with them. However, she lives a predictable life and is overcommitted, stressed, and bored with herself. Although she wishes to have a more exciting life, she feels she can never change her life routine because her children would feel neglected.

During our coaching session, she revealed some of her thoughts.

Nicole:

- *If something bad happens to the children while I am away, I could never forgive myself.*

- *My children love their father, and they would never accept another man in their lives.*

- *Fun will distract me from taking care of my children.*

- *I can wait until the children are older to take time for myself.*

Towanna: *Which of these thoughts stand out as negative chatter?*

Nicole: *All of them are negative chatter. Each of these is full of guilty feelings because I want to take time out for me.*

Case Study: Carol

Review: Carol dreams of owning her own day spa. However, she lacks the time and energy to develop her business plan. Carol gets depressed and feels like a failure because she realizes she is not living the vision for her life.

Carol is surrounded by positive people, and they encourage her to follow her vision for her life. During Carol's coaching session, she revealed the following thoughts from her chatterbox.

Carol:

- *Starting a business is hard work and takes a lot of time I do not have.*

- *I am afraid I will not be successful.*

- *I will be so busy that I'll never have time for my boyfriend and family.*

- *The bank will never loan me the money to start the business.*

- *I have the perfect location for opening the day spa, but it is too expensive.*

Towanna: *Which of these thoughts stand out as negative chatter?*

Carol: *I am feeling negative when I say that I am afraid I will not be successful. Saying those words brings me down and keeps me from wanting to try. I love spending time with my family and boy-friend. The thought of being too busy also brings me down and keeps me from wanting to try.*

Step 4.1: What fears are there between you and your goals?

____

____

____

____

____

____

____

____

____

____

____

____

Once you become aware of and recognize the distracting, non-supportive, and downright negative thoughts that you have been automatically thinking, you will be able take control and challenge their validity, or choose to eliminate them altogether. One form of taking control is practicing meditation—what is also known as reflection.

There are various forms of meditation, which is a useful way to start taking control of the mind. It enables you to take charge, slow the mind, and observe your thoughts in a detached manner so that you can control your thinking.

Meditation will help you do the following:

- Relax and quiet your mind
- Turn off irrational thinking
- Live with more balance in your life
- Live in the present moment
- Reduce toxic emotions like stress and worry

For additional information on meditation, visit the following Web sites:

- www.helpguide.org/mental/stress_relief_meditation_yoga_relaxation.htm
- www.thechristianmeditator.com

Reflection

While working through this book, you will be able to change your thinking (and feelings) from negative to positive, away from what you do not want and toward what you do want, with greater ease and with a deeper understanding of why it is necessary. When the negative chatter begins, you will quickly recognize these opposing thoughts, be able to catch yourself, and redirect your thinking toward your goal.

What Can Prevent You from Achieving Your Goal?

Asking the right questions can change your mindset from limiting to empowering. Empowering questions not only provide our minds with focus but with incentive and direction as well.

As soon as you ask a question, your mind immediately begins searching for the answer. If you don't like the answers that you are getting, it probably has a lot to do with the questions you are asking. By asking the right questions, you can empower yourself to change any area of your life.

In chapter 3, you completed the Life Balance Wheel, which enabled you to make informed and clear decisions about at least one area of your life you wish to improve. While on the journey to live a purposeful life, you will experience a problem or two. You will find things are not turning out the way you expected.

Instead of getting upset, resisting, and trying to figure out what is wrong, what went wrong, or how it went wrong, it is far more powerful to ask for the lesson, gift, and opportunity in the situation.

You will find that either the situation disappears or the difficulties dissolve, and you are moved toward your goals much more quickly. The answers come rapidly at times, and sometimes the answer takes a while. You may have to ask yourself the question repeatedly before a viable answer evolves. The answer may require learning a new skill, and therefore the resolution may take time.

You need to go outside the realm of what you already know to get new ideas, inspiration, or intuition to allow these ideas to come to you. We all have gut feelings, hunches, and ideas that pop into our minds while in the shower, exercising, or when focused on something other than the problem at hand. Many successful people trust and act on these feelings and intuitions, as they are wired to seek solutions and do not dwell on problems.

Learn to be solution—oriented and ask questions that direct you toward what you want. Some useful empowering questions to ask are:

- What is the best use of my time right now?
- What would make today a great day?
- Is this for my highest good and greatest well-being?

- How can I be most efficient with my time?
- How can I have more fun?
- What will resolve this matter?
- In what ways can I improve?
- How can I further enhance my performance?
- How can I be more professional?
- What is working right in my life?

Another set of questions can be reframes, or flips, of current questions. An example of reframes is presented in the following diagrams.

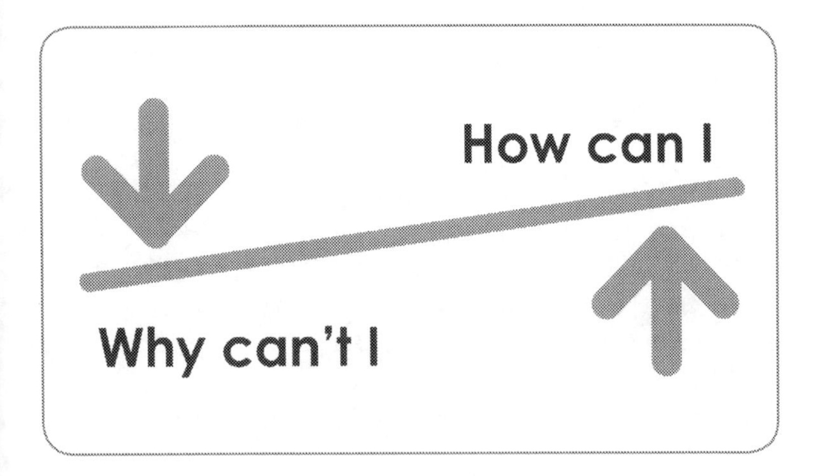

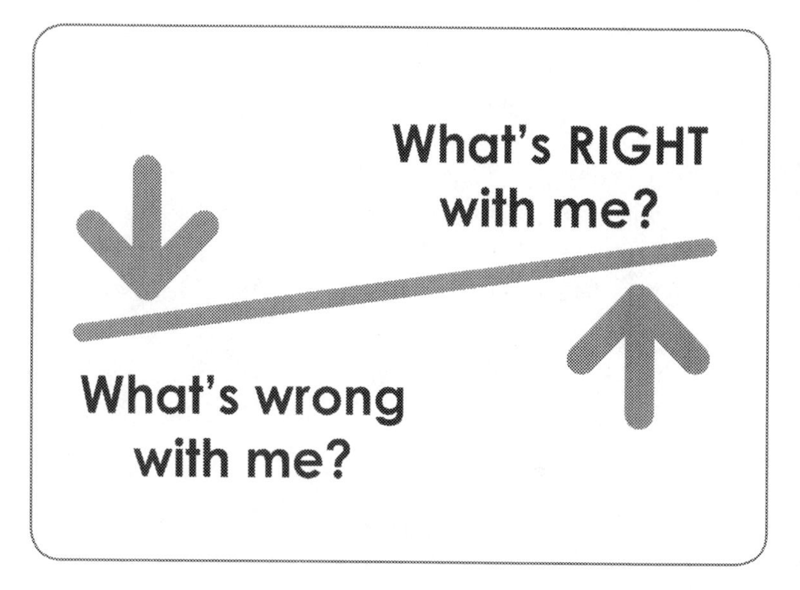

Another set of questions can be reframes, or flips, of current questions. An example of reframes is presented in the following diagrams.

You will find that the more you ask yourself empowering questions, the more empowered your life will become; and answers will come more clearly and quickly, which will enable you to continue moving in the direction you want, in order to achieve your dreams, goals, and desires.

Case Study: Nicole

Review: During Nicole's coaching session, she revealed thoughts of guilt and negative feelings. Nicole realized she wanted to change her mind-set from limiting to empowering, and she wanted support and guidance from the coaching process to make it happen. Therefore, Nicole was asked the following questions one by one so that she could focus her thoughts:

Towanna:

- *Who can you trust with your children while you are away?*

- *If you decide to introduce your children to the new man in your life, what activities can you do as a group to break the ice?*

- *Why will having fun and excitement in your life distract you from taking care of your children?*

As Nicole thought about these questions, she started to feel better, she was able to see a new perspective, and she became aware of the many choices she had available to her.

She gained confidence in her ability to improve the fun and excitement area of her life.

Nicole: *I'm a good mom, and I know that if I have plans to go out, I can still take great care of my children, and nothing could distract me from being their mom. I also know that I don't want to wait for my children to get older before I have fun. I believe that if I feel better about myself, my children will benefit from my new energy.*

In this session, Nicole made a significant step toward living an abundant and purposeful life. The feeling of guilt was gone. She changed her mind about herself and believed it in her heart. She decided that her new life would not affect her children. Now she could move forward.

Case Study: Carol

Review: Carol's chatterbox was full of limiting beliefs. She could only see the obstacles between her reality and the vision of owning a day spa, as if there were a huge mountain before her that she could not climb.

Carol is educated and has the mindset of an entrepreneur. To move her forward, she was asked the following questions:

Towanna:

- *Which aspect of the business will not be successful?*

- *Your boyfriend is supportive of your vision and enjoys spa hopping with you. What additional role could he play?*

- *If the bank denies you a loan, what other resources are available to you?*

- *Where is the next best location for the day spa?*

With each question, Carol began writing down her answers. As she pondered the answers, she became aware that what used to be obstacles between her reality and her vision were now stepping-stones for opportunity and expansion.

Carol felt free, and she was no longer afraid. In fact, she felt compelled to move forward. She was now a woman on the road to accomplishing her vision.

Carol changed her mind about herself and believed it in her heart. She decided that her business goals would not interfere with her personal time with her family and boyfriend.

To complete the following steps, refer back to your answers in step 4.1, where you listed thoughts that keep you from moving forward with your vision for your life. For each thought, complete the following exercise:

Step 5.1: What is another way of looking at this negative situation?

Step 5.2: What action can you take to move beyond this negative thought and closer to your desired goal?

Step 5.3: Ask yourself other empowering questions. Begin your questions with *How? Why? What?* For examples, refer to the list of empowering questions listed earlier in this chapter.

Reflection

Practicing empowering questions each day helps your reticular activating system (the part of your brain that acts like a spam filter on your computer) be open and focused, while seeking out the right circumstances, people, and events to guide you to your goals in the shortest possible time.

What Are Your Personal Investments?

Goals give you direction and purpose - a reason to get up early in the morning and go to bed late at night. They put drive and passion into your life. Not having goals is similar to driving across country without a map of where you are going. Goals, like maps, help you get to your destination much quicker and easier than roaming through life aimlessly. How do you know which direction to go in if you do not know where the destination is?

We all know about the importance of having goals. We set them and many of us have been successful in achieving them. As women, our greatest challenge is finding time to sit down and think about what we want to accomplish in life.

We have busy lives and a multitude of obligations and errands, which leaves very little time for us. And even when we are not busy, we might just feel more like relaxing with friends, playing computer games, or watching a movie or television. Did you know most people put far more time into planning a vacation, a family event, or a festive dinner than thinking about or even trying to make a plan for their lives!

If you wrote down your vision for your life in chapter 1, you probably already have a good idea of what you want to do. Or maybe you have done this exercise before, but you have not updated your goals for a while. Now is the time to do it.

Goals give you a real road map to your future. They provide something to strive for - a point in the future to reach. What exactly is a goal, and how do you know when you have achieved it?

A goal is a well-defined plan that gives you clarity, direction, motivation, and focus by doing the following:

- Making a positive change in your life.
- Improving or developing a skill, talent, or ability.
- Improving your performance on a task or activity.
- Forming a new routine or changing an existing routine.

Planning for your future is very important, even if those plans may change. Goals may be either short-term or long-term. Long-term goals can potentially take years, while short-term goals can be reached in weeks or months. Short-term goals are often stepping-stones along the way to our long-term goals.

Long-term goals may seem overwhelming when you do not even know where to get started. This is why we advise you to break long-term goals down into small goals that are more realistic and believable from where you are now.

To set goals effectively, it is best to write them down. The simple act of writing down your goal is so important because it takes it out of the realm of your imagination and gives it a physical representation. The act of writing the goal on paper engages your subconscious mind and emotions so that your goal has intention and purpose attached to it. You can then create a detailed plan of action.

Goals can take you toward something you want … or away from something you do not want. Therefore, write your goal in the positive and make it toward what you want.

You will sometimes find that it is easier to think about what you do not want rather than what you do want. No matter the case, it is important to convert your goals into a positive direction.

Finally, make sure they are your goals. You will be much more motivated to achieve goals that are truly yours, rather than goals that are imposed on you by someone else, like your parents, spouse, or society.

Your desire will become the fuel you need to keep yourself motivated and excited about becoming the woman who naturally has all the things listed above. Therefore, set goals that will excite your imagination and pull you forward.

Case Study: Nicole

Review: Nicole is feeling better about her decision to improve the fun and excitement in her life. She is no longer feeling guilty about taking time for herself.

With her vision in her mind, Nicole was instructed to write a list of fun and exciting activities she would like to do. Without any hesitation, Nicole completed the list.

- *Take salsa and meringue dance lessons.*

- *Travel domestically once each quarter of the year.*

- *Join a social networking group like a book club.*

It was obvious that Nicole had thought about this question before now.

However, she never took purposeful action to fulfill the vision because of the guilt she had about leaving her children.

Towanna: *Review each of the activities again and determine if any of them are long-term goals - goals that would require a year or more to accomplish.*

Nicole: *I know that traveling domestically once each quarter will take some time. Today I can afford at least two trips a year, but four trips would require me to restructure my annual budget.*

Case Study: Carol

Review: Carol is no longer afraid to move forward with her vision to own a day spa. For her next coaching session, Carol was instructed to find her business journal and review her notes.

During the session, Carol wrote a list of activities she needed to accomplish to complete the business plan.

- *Determine my start-up costs, including a sample start-up budget for a small spa.*
- *Find out what the licensing requirements are.*
- *Explore ownership options (e.g., buying an established spa, spa franchising, buying a new spa, mobile spa ...).*

- *Learn what equipment is needed and whether the equipment should be leased or purchased.*

Carol is motivated and determined. Her business journal helped her visualize what she wanted and organize her activities for purposeful action.

Towanna: *Identify any long-term goals on your list of activities.*

Carol *(after pondering for a few minutes)*: No, *these are definitely short-term goals. I believe I can work through all these activities within ninety days.*

Step 6.1: With your vision in mind, write a list of activities to start your road map.

____

____

____

____

____

____

____

____

____

____

____

____

Step 6.2: Review each of the activities and highlight any that are long-term goals - ones that would require a year or more to accomplish.

Step 6.3: Are these activities working toward a goal you want? Will these activities form a new routine or change an existing routine in your life?

Reflection

Your plan of action must be realistic in order for you to follow it. You must be able to work each step day by day, building a level of self-confidence and faith that is unshakable.

When Do You Want to Accomplish This Goal?

Many of us have heard the expression "Work smarter, not harder." There is also a belief that the harder you work, the more you are likely to accomplish. Yet in our society, we see so many people working hard and not ever achieving what they really want. The truth is that you have to do both: work smart and hard.

Working smart is planning your activities with the end in mind, while looking for the best use of your time and energy. Working hard means being dedicated, focused, and prepared to do what it takes to get and maintain the desired result. If you simply work smart to accomplish an activity, it is likely that you will relax and believe everything will maintain itself.

For example, in career development and business, when you set your goal on a promotion and you achieve it, that is working smart. However, the work does not stop there.

When Do You Want to Accomplish This Goal?

The day-to-day activities require your undivided attention to meet the expectations of your supervisors.

Another example of working smart and hard is personal weight loss. Since there is not a magic weight loss pill, you plan your meals and weight loss activities. Maintaining your desired weight also takes dedication, focus, and preparedness. It is much easier to be a couch potato when you are tired or not willing to go outside to work out when it is cold, raining, and dark outside.

In order to generate these kinds of important changes and growth in your life, you must avoid procrastination. Many procrastinators create a lot of work, look busy, and are highly active, but they are not productive toward their desired results. They are stuck in a rut. Instead, work to define and prioritize activities that build a bridge to move you closer to your goal. Focus your energies on your goals until they are achieved and continue to focus your energies to maintain your goals.

When you set goals, use the SMART acronym to assist you. SMART is a learning aid used in project management to identify the goals and objectives of a specific project. SMART stands for *specific, measurable, attainable, relevant,* and *timely.*

Specific

Your goals should be as clear and exact as possible. You have a much greater chance of achieving a specific goal than a vague and unclear goal. Clarity leads to power and success. Your subconscious mind is very literal.

Ask yourself questions like the following:

- Who is involved?

- What is required?

- When do I want it completed?

- Where is it going to happen?

Become aware of the chatterbox and develop some supportive self-talk to drown out and replace any negative non-supportive thinking. This supportive self-talk is called affirmations.

Affirmations are positive statements, written in the present tense, that you say to yourself to condition your mind. They can be in the form of a statement, a prayer, a thank-you, or a question. For example:

- I am doing something great today.

- I am happy, healthy, wealthy, and wise, now and always.

- There is plenty of time for everything.

Instead of allowing your mind to indulge in the usual disaster predictions for your future or complaints about long-gone past events, you have unlimited possibilities and choices for affirmations and encouraging self-talk.

Your words are thoughts materialized or crystallized into powerful sound waves. So, speak faith! What are you putting out into the universe? The faith you speak is what you get.

When Do You Want to Accomplish This Goal?

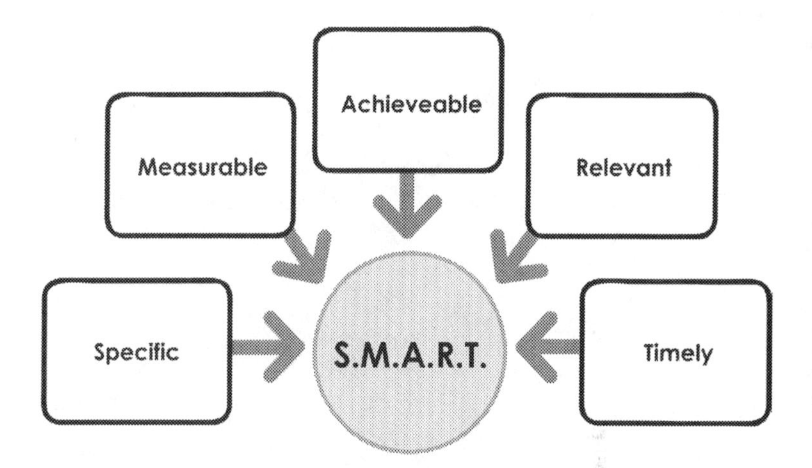

Listen to your self-talk about your goals, and if it consists of complaints, frustrations, or is repeatedly negative, you may wish to modify what you are saying. There is an old maxim: "If you can't say anything good, don't say anything at all." Now it is time to apply it to you.

Measurable

How will you measure your success? Each task toward your goal should be measurable. When you measure your progress, you stay on track. Here are sample questions you can ask yourself:

- How much time and resources are required?
- How will I know when I have reached my goal?

Since the subconscious mind does not understand loss or gain, you will need to state exactly what you are expecting. For example: "I want to train for nineteen weeks to walk a marathon (26.2 miles) by my thirtieth birthday."

Achievable

"If you believe it, you can achieve it." Many of us have heard this great quote. However, set goals that are challenging but achievable. Set goals that are realistic for your current situation and skill set.

Goals should energize and motivate you. If the goal is too extreme for your current situation and skill set, the goal may go unfulfilled and may discourage you. The following are sample questions to ask oneself:

- Is my goal realistic?
- Is my goal achievable now?
- Do I have all the skills needed to manifest this?
- Do I need to grow, stretch, learn, or heal some things to help myself along the way to my vision?
- Is there space for my goals?

Many people set goals but are often too busy or afraid to be willing to receive them. Remember the basic formula: ask, believe, and receive.

If your goal does require a certain skill set—for example, becoming a doctor, speaker, dancer, great athlete, or an investor—please go learn those skills. Take action and keep taking what motivational speaker, author, and success coach Jack Canfield calls "inspired action," until you have what you want. Taking inspired action is part of the believing and receiving section, and in doing so, you are telling the universe that you are willing, prepared, and ready to receive.

Relevant

Is your goal a passion of yours? You can have any goal you want, but if it is not a true passion, is it at least truly relevant to your life and worth your time and energy?

When a goal is also a passion, you will find endless strength and enthusiasm to succeed and keep going, even through the rough times.

Timely

The usual left-brain goal-setting techniques suggest that you put a timeframe-a deadline-around your goals and many people like to give their goals a definite date. We partly agree. Holistic goal setting and using the visualizations and affirmations are all about having your desired reality now, as if it is already in existence. So, we qualify it this way:

If your goal already has form, then set a date. If you are starting a business, you can set dates. If you are conducting seminars, then you can set dates. If you are getting married, arranging a vacation, cleaning out a closet, or having a party, then you can set dates and work toward them.

If your goal is still a dream, rather than setting a date, we suggest working with visualizations and affirmations to attract your goal. Suppose you want to win a Nobel Prize, meet and marry the ideal partner, find the house of your dreams, or do something else that is not tangible.

You could visualize the certain event or situation, as if it is already in existence.

If you feel compelled to assign a date, we suggest that you write the date with this qualifier: or *sooner*. This will allow the universe and your subconscious mind to bring it to you as quickly as possible.

Please be aware that if you have nominated a specific time frame, it could put undue pressure on you. Some people perform well under pressure and need that intensity to become focused and take action; for others, it could encourage non-supportive thinking habits to infiltrate, such as fear, worry, panic, and feeling rushed.

Be conscious of your thoughts. You cannot attract something to you by focusing or worrying about the opposite!

If you do miss your date, determine whether it was because of the following:

- Your goal was not aligned with your true values, higher purpose, or passion.

- Your goal was bigger than you originally thought.

- You have changed your desires.

If you do not attain your goal by the time you realistically chose, there is a reason. Reevaluate the goal:

- What do you want?

When Do You Want to Accomplish This Goal?

- Why do you want it?
- Is this for your higher good?

You may be surprised by your answers, and you will always find that out of adversity comes some great learning, opportunity, gift, or growth.

Case Study: Nicole

Review: Nicole listed three activities that would bring more fun and excitement to her life. Of the three activities, two were short-term goals that would take less than one year to complete.

Nicole's specific goal was to take salsa and meringue dance lessons at a dance studio or recreation center close to her home. She wanted to start the lessons in thirty days.

To make her goal measurable, Nicole calculated that the best days and times for taking time for herself would be Monday or Wednesday from 5 PM to 7 PM and Saturday from 9 AM to 1 PM. She also listed friends she could trust to come over and babysit if the dance studio she chose did not have a day care center.

To ensure the goal was achievable, Nicole was asked:

Towanna: *Is there space in your life for your goal?*

Nicole *(responding quickly): Yes! I can do it. This will fit into my schedule.*

It was fantastic to hear her respond so quickly and with so much positive energy because that meant the goal was relevant to her.

Towanna: *Okay, you have decided to find a dance class within thirty days.*

If you discover that all the classes are filled on the days you have available, what is your plan?

Nicole: *Hmmm ... I will have to wait until my son's soccer season is over. His schedule determines my availability right now.*

Towanna: *How do you feel about waiting?*

Nicole: *It's okay. To keep my commitment to myself, I will sign up for the next available class that falls after soccer season.*

Towanna: *Wonderful, Nicole! What a great way to maintain your commitment and keep yourself accountable.*

Case Study: Carol

Review: Carol wanted to complete the business plan to own a day spa. She identified four activities she needed to accomplish in ninety days to move her closer to her vision.

To make her goal measurable, Carol had to identify how much time she could commit to this effort. Carol reviewed her schedule and determined that Saturdays and lunch breaks during the workweek were the best days and times to work on these activities.

When Do You Want to Accomplish This Goal?

To decide if this goal was achievable, Carol was asked, "Is there space in your life for your goal?" A concerned look came over Carol's face, and she paused to think.

Carol: *Saturday is the primary day I spend with my boyfriend, and I just replaced him with business goals.*

This personal sacrifice did not feel good to Carol, and she wanted to make a change. Carol believed her boyfriend was more relevant than her business goals. What an important revelation! Since relationships rated high on her Life Balance Wheel, Carol did not want to change that.

Towanna: *What other days or times during your week can you find time?*

Carol: *I can use my lunch hour during the workweek and leave Saturdays for my boyfriend. But my daily lunch hour is not enough time to meet the target date.*

Towanna: *How much more time do you want to give yourself to ensure success?*

Carol: *I will extend my target date from ninety days to one hundred and eighty days. I am more comfortable with that. My lunch hour is perfect.*

Towanna: *Fantastic, Carol! How do you want me to hold you accountable to this goal?*

Carol: *Send me an e-mail each week to see if I kept my commitment.*

Towanna: *Sounds good. I will e-mail you on Sundays.*

Both Nicole and Carol found the answers within themselves. Each was able to work through the obstacles to ensure she stuck to her plan of action.

Step 7.1: Visualize what it would be like to have your goals now. Make the experience as real as possible.

____

____

____

____

____

____

____

What do you see?

____

____

____

____

____

____

____

____

When Do You Want to Accomplish This Goal?

What are you feeling?

____

____

____

____

____

____

____

____

____

____

What would you hear?

____

____

____

____

____

____

____

____

____

____

What would you smell, taste, and touch?

When Do You Want to Accomplish This Goal?

Reflection

Your plan of action is a list of goals (actionable steps) that you want to accomplish in order to generate the results you want. Your plan of action also indicates how you will accomplish each goal.

Goal Setting

Now it is your turn. In the following pages, we have provided a series of questions to assist you with brainstorming your plan of action, which will lead you to developing your SMART goals. Refer back to your list of activities from chapter 3 (step 3.3) to begin this module.

Purposeful Action

Date

Goal Setting

Area 1 (Life Balance Wheel):

What do you want?:

Why do you want it?:

What are your strengths and opportunities?:

What can prevent you from achieving your goal? :

What are your personal investments (e.g., time, money ...)?

What additional training and education do you need?

Who can help you, and what is their role?

When do you want to accomplish this goal?

Purposeful Action

Goal Setting

Date

Area 2 (Life Balance Wheel):

What do you want?:

Why do you want it?:

What are your strengths and opportunities?:

What can prevent you from achieving your goal? :

What are your personal investments (e.g., time, money ...)?

What additional training and education do you need?

Who can help you, and what is their role?

When do you want to accomplish this goal?

Purposeful Action

Goal Setting

Date

Area 3 (Life Balance Wheel):

What do you want?:

Why do you want it?:

What are your strengths and opportunities?:

What can prevent you from achieving your goal? :

What are your personal investments (e.g., time, money ...)?

___

___

___

___

___

___

___

___

___

___

___

What additional training and education do you need?

___

___

___

___

___

___

___

___

___

Who can help you, and what is their role?

When do you want to accomplish this goal?

Keep Moving Forward

Congratulations! You took the journey to make your vision a reality. Think about how much you have learned about yourself. You recognized and reprioritized your life goals to create a plan of action that focused your conscious mind, changed your limiting beliefs, and reprogrammed your subconscious mind with empowering thoughts to move you forward and achieve your goals. Although this book was designed to carefully and efficiently step you through the process of creating a plan of action for your life, you empowered yourself to make your own choices and decisions. This is worth celebrating.

Remember, your vision is what motivates you. It is only when you decide to take action to bring your vision into your reality that you will develop a clear and concise plan.

Your plan of action is a list of goals (actionable steps) that you need to accomplish in order to generate the results you want. Your plan of action also provides how you will accomplish each goal.

For you to follow it, your plan of action must be realistic. You must be able to work each step day by day, building a level of self-confidence and faith that is unshakable. Your action plan is your pathway to purpose, which leads you to your life of happiness, contentment, and fulfillment.

Regardless of the obstacles that fall in your path, continue to ask yourself the six key empowering questions that will keep you moving forward to achieving your goals:

1. What will make me happy?

2. What event brought me to this decision?

3. What are my strengths and opportunities?

4. What can prevent me from achieving my goal?

5. What are my personal investments?

6. When do I want to accomplish this goal?

To develop a more detailed plan of action, follow the SMART goal process and write additional actionable steps as a way to stay focused and stay in touch with your vision for your life.

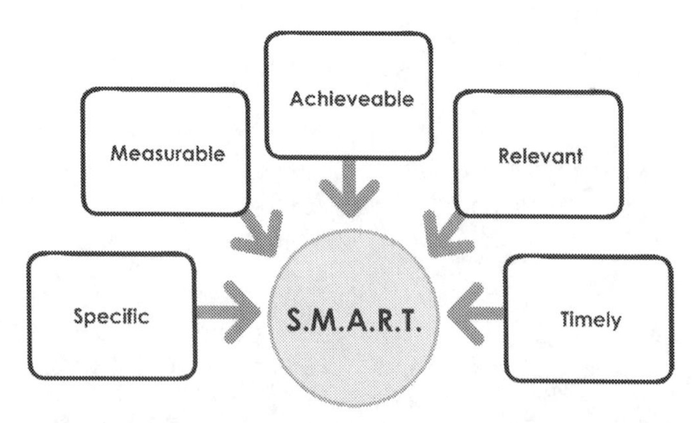

You will note that we have introduced new empowering questions to keep you moving forward:

Step 9.1: Specific

What do you want?:

____

____

____

____

Why do you want it?:

____

____

____

____

When do you want it?:

____

____

____

____

Where do you want it?:

____

____

____

____

Who can help you, and what is the role they will play?

Step 9.2: Measurable

What are your strengths and opportunities?

What can prevent you from achieving your goal?

What can prevent you from achieving your goal?

What are your personal investments (e.g., time, money ...)?

____

____

____

____

Step 9.3: Achievable

Is there space in your life for this goal?

____

____

____

____

What additional training and education do you need?

____

____

____

____

What can prevent you from achieving your goal?

____

____

____

____

Step 9.4: Relevant

Is your goal a passion?

____

____

____

____

Step 9.5: Timely

What is your time frame for achieving your goal?

____

____

____

____

Step 9.6: What additional thoughts are you experiencing at this time to motivate yourself in the future?

____

____

____

____

7 Steps to Fulfillment

When you purchased this book, you took the first step in developing your plan of action for living an abundant and purposeful life. However, we must remind you that you are not making a New Year's resolution. You are setting goals for your life. Effective goals are more than just thinking or stating a "wish" aloud. They require actually taking action steps toward achievement, putting pen to paper, and beginning the process.

This book is not designed to give you a quick fix or an overnight miracle, although for some of you, it might do that. Whoever you are, if you feel that there are changes you would like to make, now is your time.

You can create a step-by-step action plan. However, you cannot plan how fate will bring your goals to you. Your job is to focus on what you want, being open to the surprises and shortcuts that may come your way to help you achieve your results quicker and easier.

Trust that your goal is coming, prepare yourself, and be ready and willing to receive it when it shows up. How do you do this? You do this by incorporating what we call the Seven Steps to Fulfillment into your daily routine.

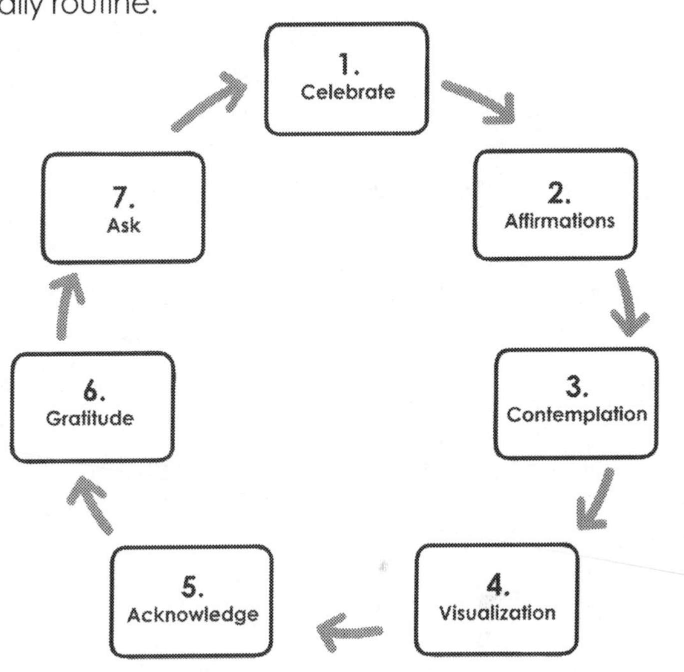

1. Celebrate

The first step is to take time to celebrate. We know you are wondering *What am I celebrating?* You are celebrating your success as if the goal has already occurred. Feel the energy of relief, joy, and acceptance. This helps reprogram your subconscious mind. Get excited and jump for joy! This may feel strange at first. But remember, this is your time to realize your full potential. The law of attraction states that *like attracts like*. You are building your momentum.

2. Affirmations

Affirmations are statements you say to yourself to condition your mind. They can be in the form of a statement, a prayer, a thank-you, or a question.

You can use one affirmation for thirty days, one per week, or a different one for each day of the week. Whichever way you choose to do it is all up to you. The affirmations will work. Choose the ones that give you the most drive.

Imprinting an affirmation into your subconscious mind, so that it becomes a belief system, requires that you repeat the affirmation many, many times over—a memorization technique called rote learning, similar to when you learned the multiplication table as a child. Even if you do not actually believe it while you are saying it, repetition will make it a part of your belief system.

Examples of affirmations:

- I am always in the right place at the right time, for the highest good of all concerned.

- Good things are happening to me now, easily and joyously.

- I am doing something great today.

- I am happy, healthy, wealthy, and wise, now and always.

- There is plenty of time for everything.
- I am surrounded by love and beauty, and I am safe in the world.
- I am a genius, and I apply my wisdom now.
- Opportunity is everywhere.
- I have everything I need, when I need it, easily, happily, harmoniously.
- I am prosperous now.
- I enjoy and deserve abundance.
- I am tremendously successful now.

3. Contemplations

Learning to focus your mind and developing the ability to concentrate does not have to be hard work. Do you remember a time when you were completely absorbed in an activity? For example, reading a good book, watching a great movie, watching and listening to your favorite musician in concert, or even staring out of a window, thinking or daydreaming, when suddenly something snaps you out of it? You were concentrating in an easy and relaxed manner; your mind was focused without stress.

Contemplation trains the mind to pay attention and gives you the ability to remain focused on a particular subject. As an added benefit, this exercise will give you greater insight to whatever you explore.

It will sharpen and strengthen your mind and allow your intuition to guide you and give you its creative input.

Insights and wisdom from your subconscious mind will also be more easily heard and understood because of your ability to contemplate and concentrate.

Remember, your subconscious mind is your "goal-seeking missile"; it will provide you with strategies and directions to best achieve your goals.

4. Visualizing

In this fourth step, you will focus all your senses to visualize what it would be like to have your goals now. Make the experience as real as possible. Remember, the subconscious mind does not know the difference between a real and vividly imagined event, so make it as real as you can by imagining colors, feelings, sounds, smells, tastes, and touches.

Imagine your goal in the present moment, not as some future event. Below we provide sample questions that will assist you with visualization.

What do you see?

- Imagine the scene: the buildings, the places, the office, the state, or the country.

- What do you see daily? Are you surrounded by family, staff members, large audiences, or a computer screen?

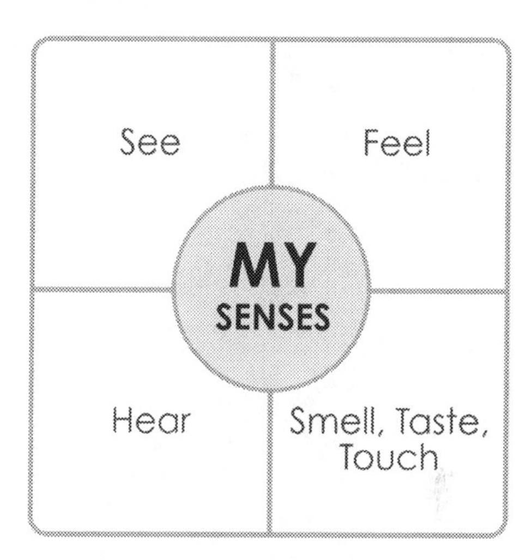

- How do you look? What clothes are you wearing?
- Are you on a cruise, vacationing around the world, receiving an award, shopping, or having dinner with friends or family?

What are you feeling?

- Are you feeling excited, exhilarated, joyous, proud, relieved, relaxed? Describe the feelings associated with the accomplishment of your goals.

What do you hear?

- Do you hear music, laughter, applause? The voices of your friends and family congratulating you?
- People asking to buy your product or services?
- Waves crashing on the sand?

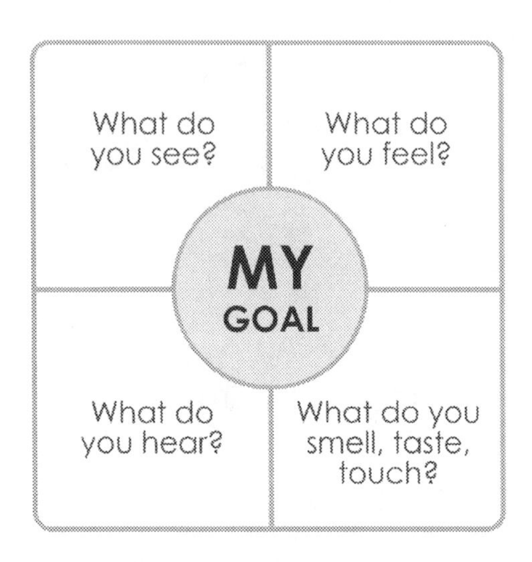

- Popping of champagne corks?
- Your name over the loudspeakers as you receive an award?

What do you smell, taste, and touch?

- Are you having a celebration meal?
- Can you imagine the smell and taste of the food and drinks you are enjoying?
- Can you imagine the fragrances, perfumes, and colognes of the people you are with?
- How about the smell of the flowers you received, a new car, or the fresh outdoors?

As you answered the questions, were you afraid to believe in what you saw? Maybe you were afraid to get your hopes up just in case it doesn't work out. Well, if it does not work out, then what have you lost? According to the Bible (Mark 9:23), All things are possible to him who believes.

So get your hopes up and believe! Make the movie as real and as detailed as you can. You will find this becoming easier as you practice it often. Without a vision, the people perish (Proverbs 29:18).

5. Acknowledge

This helps with the first belief: *Success breeds success.* Listing your successes adds to your momentum, and it is a well know psychological principle that what you focus on expands. As you think about previous success, you are programming yourself for future success. Nothing succeeds like success!

The second belief: *Like attracts like.* Thinking precisely about the things you want, surround yourself with like-minded people who have the kind of life you want to live. Go to lunch with them; attend seminars and meetings with them. If these like-minded people are not physically accessible, listen to their tapes and read their books.

6. Gratitude

Being grateful for what you already have will send out a strong signal into the universe and attract more.

Imagine how thankful you will be when your dreams do come true, some in truly miraculous ways. Whatever you have now was once a thought or maybe a dream that has come true. Develop an "attitude of gratitude" for powerful manifestation.

7. Ask

Words are the most powerful things in the universe. God created man, heaven, and Earth with his words, and the power of his words were manifested in the physical realm.

In the beginning was the Word, and the Word was with God, and the Word was God. And the Word was made flesh, and dwelt among us (John 1:1).

In this final step, you will list your goals. What do you want to happen? You will consciously create your day this way. Ask for what you want for today or for your life. This creates your intention for what you want to happen.

Purposeful Plan

The process of creating a purposeful plan of action for your life takes discipline and focus on what matters most to you. Refer back to any of the information outlined previously. The key is to write down your answers. This will allow the process to build on itself, and you will do a better job.

Always empower yourself by surrounding yourself with positive friends, family, colleagues, and anything that will keep you in touch with yourself and what is most important to you. Additionally, if you do not have a life coach, it is a good idea to find someone who will hold you accountable for completing your plan of action. You can have greater success if there is a person whom you can meet with on a regular basis to check on your progress and support you when things get tough.

Even after you have executed what appears to be a flawless plan of action, you may experience failures. When failures occur, remember that there is a reason.

Reevaluate the goal by asking yourself the following questions:

- What do I want?
- Why do I want it?
- Is this for my higher good?

Your answers may surprise you. However, out of adversity comes some great learning, opportunity, gift, or growth.

Purposeful Environment

Create a special place for yourself. Make it a comfortable and productive environment. Clear your desk, sit in the park, go to the library, or go to the beach. It is important to eliminate distractions. Remember to turn off your phones, and you definitely need to put the kids to bed or start the plan of action while everyone is away for a few hours.

Purposeful Goal Setting

Make a cup of coffee or tea, turn on some music, and start writing your goals. This may take you several hours or several days.

No matter how long it takes you to complete your goal setting, the key is getting it done.

Purposeful Action

Once you have written your goals using the SMART method, you will develop your completion strategy by incorporating your goals into a thirty-day journal and following the Seven Steps to Fullfilment. At the end of this book, we have provided you with three days of journaling pages with the seven steps outlined.

How to Use the Journaling Pages

When you write down your first goal (refer back to chapter 8), follow the Seven Steps to Fulfillment:

1. Celebrate: Do so as if the goal has already occurred.

2. Affirmation: Write your favorite affirmation and say it aloud or to yourself, ten to one hundred times throughout the day. Emotional and enthusiastic repetition will help it quickly become part of your belief system. Remember, if you feel any resistance to these statements, ask yourself an empowering question (refer back to chapter 4).

3. Contemplation: Spend a consistent five minutes focusing, thinking, considering, wondering, asking questions. The quality of your questions will direct the quality of your life, so ask high-quality questions.

4. Visualization: Spend a continuous five minutes visualizing your goal. Make a movie in your mind, as if your goal has been achieved. Use all your senses. Make the experience as real as possible.

5. Acknowledging: List up to five successes that you have ever achieved.

6. Gratitude: List up to five people, things, or events that you already have that you can be grateful for.

7. Ask: Set your intention for the day.

Most people have all the talent, skill, awareness, and ambition they need, but it is often hidden under a cloud of self-doubt, past dissappointments, or simply being too busy.

We rarely take time to examine what we are doing or why we are doing it.

The material in this book is designed to guide, coach, and carefully step you through the process of developing a plan of action that is aligned with what you want for yourself in all aspects of your life.

Online Resources: You can purchase additional journaling pages, which are available for download at ***www.purposefulactiononline.com***

We pray that you are more successful in all that you do.

Review Checklist

❍ You have completed your Life Balance Wheel.

❍ You know which areas of your life are in balance.

❍ You have prioritized those areas in your life you want to work on first, second, third, and so forth.

❍ You have written SMART goals for each of those areas.

❍ You have assigned a timeline to complete each goal.

❍ You learned the importance of affirmations and empowering questions.

❍ You were introduced to the Seven Steps to Fulfillment, the daily process for developing the mindset for accomplishing your goals.

Daily Journal

This journal provides you with enough pages for three days. However, you may determine that you need to extend your timeline to 60, 90, or 365 days. If this is the case, make copies of the journal pages or purchase one of our supplement journals to continue the format. Repetition is the key to success.

Online Resources: You can purchase additional journaling pages, which are available for download at ***www.purposefulactiononline.com***

Day 1

Date

Goal:

Refer back to chapter 6:

Affirmation:
Choose your favorite one and say it aloud to yourself ten times now and many times throughout the day.

Acknowledge success:
Based on your goal, list up to five successes that you have achieved.

1.

2. __________

3. __________

4. __________

5. __________

Gratitude:
List one to five people, things, or events that you already have that you can be grateful for.

1. ______________________________

____

____

____

____

2. ______________________________

____

____

____

____

3. ______________________________

____

____

____

____

4. ______________________________

____

____

____

____

5.

Ask:

Write statements of what you want, as if they are already facts.

Day 2

Date

Goal:

Refer back to chapter 6:

Affirmation:

Choose your favorite one and say it aloud to yourself ten times now and many times throughout the day.

Acknowledge success:

Based on your goal, list up to five successes that you have achieved.

1.

2. ____

____

____

____

____

____

3. ____

____

____

____

____

____

4. ____

____

____

____

____

____

5. ____

____

____

____

____

Gratitude:

List one to five people, things, or events that you already have that you can be grateful for.

1. ______________________________

____

____

____

____

2. ______________________________

____

____

____

____

3. ______________________________

____

____

____

____

4. ______________________________

____

____

____

____

5.

Ask:

Write statements of what you want, as if they are already facts.

Day 3

Date

Goal:

Refer back to chapter 6:

____

____

____

____

Affirmation:

Choose your favorite one and say it aloud to yourself ten times now and many times throughout the day.

____

____

____

____

Acknowledge success:

Based on your goal, list up to five successes that you have achieved.

1. ______________________________

____

____

____

____

2. ____

____

____

____

____

____

3. ____

____

____

____

____

____

4. ____

____

____

____

____

____

5. ____

____

____

____

____

Gratitude:
List one to five people, things, or events that you already have that you can be grateful for.

1. ____

____

____

____

____

2. ____

____

____

____

____

3. ____

____

____

____

____

4. ____

____

____

____

____

5. ____________________

Ask:

Write statements of what you want, as if they are already facts.

Notes:

Notes:

The Authors

Towanna B. Freeman, CEC, DD

A career strategist and life and success coach, Towanna holds a bachelor of science degree from Howard University and an honorary doctorate in divinity. She is also a certified core energy coach.

She is also the founder of the Young Women's Empowerment Network (www.ywen.org), a non-profit organization, established in 1999, that provides educational resources, counseling services, and training to girls ages ten through eighteen.

Barbara H. Pellegrino, CEC

Trained in mind power, Barbara is a certified neuro-linguistic programming (NLP) facilitator and trainer, a certified core energy coach, an achievement life coach, leading Vision Board expert, and the author—with Dr. Wayne Dyer, Anthony Robbins, Michael Beckwith, and Bill Harris—of Living in Abundance.

Barbara conducts Vision Boards training—"Treasure Mapping Your Way to Success" workshops—and "Advanced Manifesting Skills" classes in Hawaii, Australia, and the mainland of the United States.